# THE
# EDENS
# A LEGACY
# STORY

USA TODAY BESTSELLING AUTHOR
# DEVNEY PERRY

**THE EDENS – A LEGACY STORY**

ISBN: 978-1-957376-40-0

Editing & Proofreading:

Judy Zweifel, Judy's Proofreading

Julie Deaton, Deaton Author Services

# OTHER TITLES

## The Edens Series

Christmas in Quincy - Prequel

Indigo Ridge

Juniper Hill

Garnet Flats

Jasper Vale

Crimson River

Sable Peak

## Treasure State Wildcats

Coach

Blitz

## Clifton Forge Series

Steel King

Riven Knight

Stone Princess

Noble Prince

Fallen Jester

Tin Queen

Quarter Miles

Forsaken Trail

Dotted Lines

## Calamity Montana Series

The Bribe

The Bluff

The Brazen

The Bully

The Brawl

The Brood

## Standalones

Ivy

Rifts and Refrains

A Little Too Wild

## Holiday Brothers

The Naughty, The Nice and The Nanny

Three Bells, Two Bows and One Brother's Best Friend

A Partridge and a Pregnancy

# CONTENTS

# CHAPTER ONE

## ANNE

N ew Year's Eve Eve.

Not a holiday. Not by any stretch of the imagination. Yet my friends had insisted we celebrate. That we ring in 1988 with something special.

Apparently, *something special* meant a dark, two-track gravel road in the middle of the wilderness.

"Where is this cabin?" I muttered to the windshield.

Amanda and Jessica had come to the mountains earlier today. If they were waiting for me, shouldn't I be able to see a light or something? My headlights illuminated the trail in front of me, but beyond their reach, it was pitch black. A night so dark it could swallow you whole.

A night where a woman alone could go missing, never to be seen from again.

The hairs on the back of my neck stood on end as my truck crept forward toward the tree line.

"Ted Bundy is in jail. Get a grip, Anne."

There were no serial killers waiting for me in this forest. The chill zinging down my spine was nothing more than the cold and my imagination running rampant. I'd watched too many episodes of *Unsolved Mysteries*.

Maybe New Year's Eve Eve wasn't an actual holiday, but this weekend getaway would be fun, right? A chance for me to spend quality time with my two best friends from high school.

I hadn't seen Amanda and Jessica much these past three and a half years since I'd gone to college at the University of Montana. They'd both stayed in our hometown after graduation, and with school and work, I didn't make it to Quincy often these days.

But this year, I'd wanted more time with my parents around Christmas. So with school on recess for winter break, I'd taken a week off work to enjoy the holidays. Mom and I had been shopping downtown on Christmas Eve when I'd bumped into Amanda.

We'd organized a girls' night at Willie's for a drink. I'd been in the middle of my rum and Coke when Jessica had sprung this trip on me. Slightly buzzed and lost down memory lane with my oldest friends, I'd agreed.

If I did get snatched by a serial killer, Captain Morgan was to blame.

"Ugh," I groaned, leaning closer to the wheel as my truck bounced along the bumpy road.

There weren't any tire tracks in the snow. Granted, it was snowing, but if Amanda and Jessica had come this way, shouldn't there still be tracks?

I snatched Jessica's directions, squinting to make out her notes, but the cab was too dark, so I hit the light above my head.

*Drive five miles.*
*Cabin is the first one you come to.*

2

*Green gate.*

I checked the odometer. When I'd turned off the highway, I'd set it to zero. It was only on four. Did this road even continue for another mile?

The trees were just feet away, the parting between their trunks like jaws, open wide. I gulped, forcing myself to keep my foot on the gas pedal.

When I'd left Quincy an hour ago, the stars had been out in full force, scattering the midnight sky with sparkles. The moon had cast a silver glow over the mountains and meadows. But then a thick blanket of clouds had rolled in, blocking out the sky and blotting any light.

Then the snow had started. That should have been my hint to turn back.

Fat, heavy flakes caught my headlights as they drifted to the ground. Perfect for cross-country skiing.

I hated cross-country skiing.

The last thing I wanted to do on my holiday break was exercise. But Amanda and Jessica had the whole trip planned, including an easy ski trail. So in an effort to participate, I'd unearthed my skis from Mom and Dad's garage, blown off the dust and tossed them into the back of my pickup.

Mom thought this getaway would be good for my heart. That it would give me a chance to get my mind off Jeremy.

The thief.

Talk about an epic waste of a year. I only wished I'd been the one to dump him first.

His explanation had been grating on me for weeks. *This isn't working for me anymore.* What kind of reason for ending a year-long relationship was that? Didn't I deserve

3

more? Didn't I at least deserve to have my property returned?

Jeremy had showed up at my apartment the day before finals with a box of items I'd left at his place. A sweatshirt. A notebook. The Walkman he'd borrowed for his walks to and from campus.

Except what he'd forgotten to bring me were all of my cassette tapes. Ten, to be exact.

Ten cassette tapes, loaded with my favorite songs. Ten cassette tapes, each painstakingly compiled. Some I'd had since high school. How long had it taken me to create those tapes? How many hours had I sat beside my cassette player, listening to the radio and waiting to hit record when the perfect song came on? Countless.

He'd stolen countless hours, then had the gall to lie and say they were at my house. That I'd lost them.

My hands strangled the wheel as my lip curled.

I knew exactly where those ten tapes were—on the shelf beneath his TV where I'd left them so that while we were studying in his living room, we could listen to music. He'd insisted that shelf was empty. We'd argued about it for five minutes until he'd just walked away.

The only tapes I had left were the ones I'd kept in my truck. Dolly Parton. George Jones. And one of my mom's— Amy Grant.

Jeremy had even kept my Heart tape. He hated Heart.

"Asshole," I muttered.

The radio crackled, the signal going in and out. The only decent reception this close to the mountains would be on an AM channel, but I didn't feel like listening to oldies. The news talk channel I'd had on earlier had been replaying a sound bite from President Reagan's latest address. Then they'd delved into a report on the upcoming Winter Olympics that would be held in Calgary this February.

If I was going to be ambushed by a serial killer, I'd rather go down in silence, so I turned the radio off entirely.

With every passing second, the snow seemed to fall heavier. Faster. It crunched beneath my tires. My wiper blades whipped from side to side, and my shoulders hunched closer and closer toward the wheel.

"Don't get stuck," I whispered to my 1982 Chevy Silverado. It was white, and if I got buried, no one would find me until long after I'd become a human popsicle.

The evergreens towered above me. The road narrowed. Where the hell was this cabin? My stomach twisted, my knuckles white as I stared ahead into utter darkness.

The odometer turned. Five miles.

And no cabin in sight.

"Forget this trip." I scanned the forest for a place to turn around, but as I inched past a tree, a flicker of light caught my eye.

My entire body sagged as a green gate came into view. Then came the cabin. "Oh, thank God."

A golden glow poured from its windows. Amanda's face was pressed to the glass, peering outside with her hands cupped to her eyes. When she recognized my truck, she smiled and waved wildly.

I smiled, more relief than joy, and parked beside her two-tone Ford pickup. Stretching across the bench seat, I snagged my duffel bag, purse and coat, then opened the door. My knees wobbled, nerves from the drive, and the moment my boots hit the snow, Amanda was there, her arms spread wide.

"You're finally here!" she squealed, pulling me in for a hug. "How was the drive?"

"Long," I breathed, letting her go to slam my truck door closed. The skis would stay in the back, buried beneath snow and forgotten for all I cared.

"You should have just ridden with us," she said, leading the way to the cabin.

"I know." But I needed to leave on Sunday morning to go home, pack and drive back to Missoula for my final semester. I didn't want to rush them home.

"Are you hungry?"

"Starved," I said, following her into the cabin and stomping my boots on the mat. The scent of a wood fire, tomatoes and garlic filled my nose. My stomach growled.

"Christopher made his famous stew and cornbread."

Wait. Christopher was here? "Oh. I, um . . . I didn't realize he was coming."

The sound of male voices carried from beyond the cabin's entryway as I hung my coat and purse up on a hook.

When Amanda and Jessica had invited me along, I'd assumed it was just going to be us girls. But I should have known their boyfriends would be here too. Amanda and Christopher were high school sweethearts. So were Jessica and Matthew.

Which made me the fifth wheel. *Awesome.*

If I left now, would I make it home before midnight?

No. No, I wouldn't. And tonight, I'd rather be the extra than alone on a dark highway.

Footsteps thudded on the wooden floors, then Jessica flew past Amanda, hauling me into a hug. "You're here! Finally. Hi."

"Hi." I hugged her back.

"I was starting to get worried when it took you so long,"

she said. "You didn't get lost, did you? Were my directions okay?"

"They were perfect." I nodded, letting her go. "But it started to snow, so I took it slow."

I looked past her to see Matthew and Christopher, both with a beer bottle in their hands. "Hey, guys."

Dinner. A beer. And bed. The nice thing about being the fifth wheel was that no one would notice when I slipped away early to crash.

"Hey, Anne," Christopher said.

Matthew jerked up his chin. "Glad you made it."

"Amanda was getting so nervous, she was about to send me out to find you." A deep, gravelly voice came from around the corner.

My stomach dropped.

I knew that voice. It had gotten deeper since I'd heard it last, but I knew that voice. Once upon a time, I'd loved that voice.

No. No, this couldn't be happening.

My gaze flew to Amanda.

She had the decency to look guilty.

Then Harrison Eden took the space beside Christopher, then saluted me with his own beer. "Hey, Anne."

My mouth opened. Closed. Opened. Closed. I blinked, tearing my eyes away from Harrison's annoyingly handsome face, to aim them at Jessica. "What is he doing here?"

My friends shared a look. Then Jess lifted a shoulder. "Um . . . Happy New Year's Eve Eve?"

New Year's Eve Eve. The worst non-holiday of all time.

# CHAPTER TWO

## HARRISON

Anne Snow.

It had been too damn long.

She was surprised to see me. And pissed off too. She'd never been good about schooling her features when she was mad.

Her cheeks were flushed a pretty pink, the same shade as her lips. Her bright blue eyes flared. But that anger only made her more striking. One look and my chest tightened.

There weren't many women who were so beautiful that they made it hard to breathe.

A better man would have bowed out of this trip when he'd learned his ex-girlfriend was coming along. A better man would have let her enjoy the weekend with her friends. Except I wasn't a better man. And it had been too damn long.

"What's it been? Five years?" I asked.

Her nostrils flared. "Six."

"Six. Huh." I took a sip of my beer. "If you've been counting, does that mean you've missed me?"

Anne's gaze flickered to where my ski poles were propped up against the wall beside my skis in the entryway. She stared at the metal tip like it would make the perfect weapon. "My aim is much better at close distances."

"Christopher." Amanda put her arm around Anne's shoulders while Jessica took her duffel, setting it aside. "Anne's starving."

"On it." He spun on a heel and disappeared to the kitchen where the clank of a plate and bowl echoed.

Amanda shuffled Anne past Matthew and me, acting as a buffer on their way to the kitchen.

"Maybe I should have warned her." Jessica's shoulders slumped. "Oops."

"It'll be fine," I said, tipping my beer to my lips for another swig.

This animosity between us had lasted too long anyway. It had been six years. This wasn't high school. We weren't teenagers anymore. We could be civil for a weekend, right?

Matthew pulled Jessica into his side, bending to kiss her fiery red hair, then led the way to the living room where we'd been visiting for the past few hours, waiting for Anne to arrive.

The fire we'd started earlier was roaring in the hearth, its flames keeping the log cabin toasty warm. Before Anne had gotten here, I'd been sitting on one of the four leather chairs that circled the coffee table. But as she took a seat at the dining table, with a plate, bowl and a beer of her own, I pulled out a chair beside hers.

She shot me a glare as she ate her first bite of stew.

"Hey, darlin'."

"Don't call me darlin'." She pointed her spoon at my nose.

I fought a grin. "You used to like it."

"I also used to like you. Times change." She shoveled another bite into her mouth, staring out the windows to where the snow was dumping from the sky.

"How have you been?"

She swallowed, took a drink, then ate another spoonful.

"That's great," I said, pretending like she'd answered. "I've been good too. Busy. Working on the ranch. Just about time to start calving, so I'll be pulling some long nights."

Anne blinked, then cut off a piece of yellow cornbread, dripping with melted butter and honey.

"Anne, do you want some champagne?" Amanda appeared at the table, jerking her chin for me to go to the living room, but I just smirked and settled deeper into my chair. She rolled her eyes, then held up the bottle of champagne.

"Oh, no, thanks. I'm good," Anne said. "I think I'll stick to beer."

A memory flashed in my mind, a summer night I hadn't thought about for ages.

Anne and I in the cab of my pickup, driving on the dirt roads at the ranch. She'd sat in the middle so I could put my arm around her shoulders. Her hand had rested on my thigh. And on the floorboard there was a six-pack of beer to drink while we were camping.

Granted, neither of us had been old enough to drink legally. Her parents had thought she was spending the weekend with Amanda. Mine had thought I was camping with the guys.

We'd only had a few of those camping trips, Anne and I, along with our cheap beer that I'd begged one of the ranch hands to buy me. Then, before we'd made it to another summer, Anne had dumped me.

For no damn reason.

"So did you hear about what happened to Johnny Wells?" Amanda asked, taking the chair by Anne's side.

"No, what?" Anne shifted in her chair, giving me the back of her head. The ends of her dark, silky hair tickled her waist.

It was longer by at least six inches than it had been in high school. Her face had changed too, matured. A woman's face. And a woman's body, slender yet curved in just the right places.

Jessica joined us at the table, giving me the same look to disappear. And this time, I obeyed, standing from my chair to join the guys in the living room. Mostly because there'd be time to pester Anne later.

"This is a great cabin," I told Matthew.

It was his grandfather's, built in the sixties. Remote but they had the necessities. Electricity. Running water. Indoor plumbing.

"Thanks," he said. "He doesn't spend much time here in the winter these days. He likes to be closer to town."

"Lucky for us," Christopher said. "I'm glad to be out of town for a weekend."

"Same here," Matthew said. "Though I wish he had a TV. Would be great to watch a game. I've been begging him to get one for years, but he likes to come up here and disconnect. Read."

I, for one, didn't care about a television. I rarely watched it at home, too busy working, and tonight, there was another object that had captured my interest.

Anne yawned at the table, covering it with the back of

her hand, while Amanda and Jessica kept talking, filling her in on the latest Quincy gossip. Mostly, they talked about their former classmates. Who was married. Who was divorced, already. Who was drinking too much and who'd spent a few nights in jail.

Personally, I didn't care much for the rumor mill. Unless it involved me, my family or one of our businesses, I tuned it out. And from the look of Anne's droopy eyes, her second, third and fourth yawn, she didn't care much either.

"Want another beer?" Christopher asked.

I tore my eyes from Anne, glancing to my bottle. "Yeah. Sure."

"I'm going to put another log on this fire," Matthew said, moving to the fireplace.

Anne yawned again, this time risking a glance to the living room as she covered it with a hand. When she found my gaze waiting, she glared.

I chuckled.

She'd always had spirit, even when she'd been a sophomore and I'd been a senior at Quincy High. Nothing about me had ever intimidated Anne. It was sexy as hell. Then. Now.

"I'm so tired," she told the girls. "Would you be annoyed if I went to bed early?"

Before they could answer, Anne stood from the table, carrying her empty bowl and plate to the sink. She washed them quickly, setting them to dry in the rack on the counter, then walked toward the door, disappearing for a moment before returning with her duffel bag.

But what she'd missed while she was cleaning up was the look shared between Amanda and Jessica.

A look Anne would not like.

"You can't go to bed yet," Jess said, standing. "You just got here."

"But we have all weekend, right?" Anne blew out a long breath. "That drive took it out of me. I promise, come tomorrow morning, I'll be good as new. Just point me in the direction of my pillow."

Amanda's eyes flew to Jessica's. Then they both looked to Matthew, who'd finished with the fire and was back in his chair at my side.

He cleared his voice and stood. "Yeah, uh, this cabin used to have four bedrooms. I haven't been here since the summer. Guess during hunting season this fall, Granddad decided to take one of those rooms and convert it to a reloading room."

"Okay," Anne drawled, glancing around the living room. She blinked twice, like she was just realizing there were no couches.

Apparently Matthew's grandfather preferred chairs.

"We, um, sort of have to . . . double up," Jess said.

"Double up?" Anne repeated.

"I know it sucks. But we took the smaller bedrooms," Amanda said. "They only have full-sized beds. The one in there has a queen." She pointed toward an open bedroom door off the living room.

When we'd arrived and I'd gone to take my bag to the spare bedroom, only to find empty shotgun shells strewn across a table, we'd realized there was going to be a problem.

"Wait." Anne held up a hand, staring between her friends before looking to me.

I shrugged. "I promise not to snore."

Her jaw dropped, then she snapped it closed with an audible click, before shaking her head. "No."

"Come on, Anne," I said. "It's not that big of a deal."

Her eyes cut past me, toward the bedroom.

The thought crossing her mind might as well have been written on her forehead.

She bolted, sprinting through the living room.

"Shit." I catapulted over my chair, almost knocking it over and tripping myself, but I managed to land, my socks sliding on the wood floor.

I'd been closer to the bedroom. Not by much, but closer.

We reached the door's frame at exactly the same time, both trying to squeeze through the opening. Except our bodies collided, sandwiching us together in the threshold.

Her elbow dug into my gut.

"Oof. Have you been sharpening those?"

"Sleep on the floor." She gritted her teeth, trying to wiggle inside, but I wrapped my arms around her, holding her back.

The moment she was in that room, she'd slam the door in my face and flip the lock.

"I'm not sleeping in that bed with you," she seethed.

"I'm not sleeping on the floor." I mean, I would if I had to. But these floors were rock solid. No soft woods for Matthew's granddad, instead, he'd built with rough-cut oak.

"Let me go." She thrashed, shaking my arms loose. Then with one long stride, she was in the bedroom.

I was right on her heels.

"Get out, Harrison."

I frowned. "It's not like I haven't seen you naked before."

Wrong thing to say. I realized it a moment too late.

Anne's duffel bag swung through the air and smacked me in the face. "Get. Out."

"Why is this a big deal?" I threw a hand toward the bed.

"You'll stay on your side. I'll stay on mine. We don't even have to talk. Unless you finally want to explain to me why you dumped me in high school."

Never, not once, had she given me a reason. She'd just called it off. Without warning. One day, I'd been taking her out on a date. The next, we were over.

To this day, I had no idea why. She hadn't even explained it to Amanda or Jessica.

Anne's gaze flew toward the wall, her jaw clenched.

"I'll make you a deal." A smug grin stretched across my face. Maybe I could make this work in my favor, after all. At least make the back pain from a shitty night on the floor worth it. "You tell me why you broke it off in high school. And you can have the bed all to yourself."

"I don't owe you an explanation," she clipped. "You know what you did."

"No, I don't." I had no fucking clue. But I'd done something. And she seemed intent on holding it against me for the rest of my life.

We'd dated for a year. Didn't I deserve an explanation? Well, maybe a night in the same bed would encourage her to share.

I strode forward to my bag that I'd left on the mattress earlier. Then I faked a yawn. "You know? I'm pretty tired too. Think I'll turn in."

"Harrison," she warned.

I answered by unbuttoning my shirt. The pearl snaps popped free, collar to hem.

"What's it going to be, darlin'?" I arched an eyebrow. "Talk? Or cuddle?"

Anne's lip curled. "Fine."

For a moment, I thought she'd actually talk. Finally, after six years, I'd know why she'd broken my heart.

Except she didn't open her mouth. She dropped her bag to the floor, and opened it instead, taking out a nightshirt. Then she stood and pointed a finger at my nose. "If you snore, I'll smother you with my pillow in your sleep."

# CHAPTER THREE

## ANNE

My friends were partying. They'd been partying for hours beyond the closed bedroom door while I'd been attempting to sleep—unsuccessfully.

Since my attempt to get some rest had been futile, I'd resorted to staring at the dark ceiling, listening to them laugh and talk, while dreading Harrison's return.

After our argument, he'd been wary to leave the room, knowing that I'd lock him out. So he'd threatened to take the door off its hinges. We'd been in the middle of a staredown when Amanda had finally intervened, playing mediator.

Neither Harrison nor I wanted to sleep on the floor, so we'd come to an agreement.

We'd limit the sharing hours of this stupid bed.

Harrison would leave me alone until midnight. And since I was an early riser, I'd be out of here by five.

I should be in dreamland. I should be capitalizing on my solitary mattress hours. Except I couldn't sleep, not only from the noise in the living room, but from the noise in my head.

When I'd broken up with Harrison in high school, he'd pretended he had no idea why. Like the words he'd spoken that had utterly crushed my sixteen-year-old heart had come from someone else's mouth.

I hadn't believed his clueless act, not for a second. Not even Harrison Eden got away with everything.

The Edens were Quincy royalty. His family had founded the town generations ago. You couldn't drive down Main Street without seeing at least one of his relatives. The Eden name was splashed across—or written behind—numerous businesses.

Maybe the reason Harrison had never lacked in confidence was because he and his family were so well-known. Or maybe it just came naturally for him.

Regardless of the cause, people were drawn to him. He was the sun and they were planets, blissfully circling in his orbit.

When he'd asked me out on that first date, it had been the easiest *yes* of my life. Who wouldn't want to date the most popular and good-looking guy in school? To be the girl on his arm, basking in his confidence and charisma?

Harrison had been captain of the football and basketball teams. An honor roll student. He'd even played guitar, bringing it along whenever we'd go camping to strum a tune beside the fire.

My motives for agreeing to that first date had been, admittedly, shallow. But it was his easy laugh and quick wit that had charmed me all those years ago. His playful humor. His sweet side.

I'd fallen for Harrison Eden.

I'd been duped by Harrison Eden.

Unless . . .

Was I wrong? When he'd been so shocked that I'd had the nerve to dump him, I'd dismissed it as an act. A coverup to hide his bruised ego. Heaven forbid he admit fault.

But tonight, he'd still been singing that same, tired line. That he had no idea why I'd broken up with him.

Maybe if Amanda, Jess and the boyfriends hadn't been hovering outside the door, clinging to our every heated word, I would have reminded him of exactly what he already knew.

*If* he already knew.

Did he really not have the slightest idea?

Well, I remembered every word. Women remembered the statements men used to scorn them.

*She's not a virgin anymore.*

I cringed.

Years later and I still felt grimy. Not even Amanda and Jessica knew the reason why I'd ended it with Harrison. I just hadn't been able to bring myself to repeat it. Keeping the tears hidden from my friends had been hard enough.

I'd been in love with Harrison.

And he'd just been killing time with a local virgin, biding his time during his senior year until he could leave for college.

Harrison *had* to know why I'd ended it. If I remembered, he would too. The man was as annoyingly smart as he was gorgeous.

I sighed, twisting in bed for the hundredth time, flopping on my stomach and hugging a pillow. What time was it? There was no clock on the nightstand, but with every passing heartbeat, midnight crept closer.

Then I'd be stuck with Harrison.

"Ugh." This bed wasn't big enough for us both.

Maybe I should just sleep on the floor. I could just curl up beside the fire, like I was camping.

Except that would mean giving Harrison the satisfaction of winning. My pride wouldn't allow it. A gentleman would let me have the bed to myself, but I'd learned a long time ago, despite the wool he'd pulled over everyone else's eyes, Harrison was no gentleman.

"Christopher, stop!" Amanda was laughing hysterically from the living room. It was more of a cackle now that she was likely drunk.

"What? I'm not doing anything." Christopher chuckled. "I'm just trying to cuddle."

"Get a room." Jessica giggled. "Actually, I'm going to take my own advice. Matthew?"

"That's my cue. Night, guys." Their footsteps pounded on the floor, like they were both running for their bedroom. A door slammed. Then the giggling came from beyond our shared wall.

*Great.* My friends were about to have sex, and I'd get to listen.

I snagged the pillow beside mine—Harrison's pillow—and pulled it over my head. "Why am I here?"

The pillow didn't have an answer.

Why was I here? I didn't want to go cross-country skiing. Tomorrow, of all days. I was already exhausted, and I'd been here for mere hours. School was starting again, and I needed to be fresh for my last semester.

More footsteps echoed from beyond the door, probably Amanda and Christopher disappearing to their room.

I woke up every day at five in the morning. It was why I'd been able to make the deal with Harrison to get a few hours in here alone. My natural alarm clock was precise.

If I woke up tomorrow before everyone else, I could just . . . slip away. Leave a note. Amanda and Jessica would be pissed, but I didn't really care. They'd invited Harrison knowing full well that he was enemy number one. Yes, he was friends with Matthew and Christopher, but still.

They should have picked my side. Or not invited me in the first place.

The door creaked open.

I froze, my heart scooting its way toward my throat.

He took one step into the room. Then another. My body stiffened, sensing him close to the bed. Then the pillow was ripped away from my head.

"Hey!" I sat up.

"That's mine," he grumbled, turning back for the door.

For a brief, blissful moment, I thought he'd walk out of the room. That he'd take his pillow and leave me in peace.

Nope.

He turned on the light switch.

"Do you mind?" I squinted as my eyes adjusted, glaring when he tossed the pillow to his side of the bed. "I was sleeping."

"No, you weren't." He stalked to his bag on the floor, undoing the zipper. He bent, fishing out a leather toiletry case before taking it into the adjoining bathroom, slamming the door.

My lip curled as I whipped the covers off my legs and marched for the light switch, bathing the room in darkness. Then I snuggled under the covers, taking Harrison's pillow and wedging it beneath the sheet to form a barrier.

I'd just barely settled onto my stomach again when the door to the bathroom flew open and Harrison stalked back to the light, turning it on. Again.

"Harrison," I snapped.

"Anne."

A shiver rolled down my spine at that deep, rugged tone. It shouldn't have been sexy. It was just a man's voice, speaking my name with a hint of spite.

But it was.

I sent him a glare for good measure.

He shot a return scowl over his shoulder, then reached for the hem of his shirt, dragging it over his head.

My jaw dropped. Thankfully, my pillow caught it.

Holy muscles, where had those come from? Not only had his voice matured, but it was like he'd changed his body too. Harrison had been strong in high school, but the mass he'd added to his arms, those broad shoulders, was mouth-watering.

And the abs. Oh. My. God. The abs.

Jeremy hadn't had abs like that. Maybe if he had, I wouldn't be so upset about my stolen tapes.

I was drooling over the narrow line of Harrison's waist when I realized he'd stopped moving. My eyes flew to his.

He was smirking, that arrogant, infuriating smirk, with his shirt held in his hands. "You can watch. I don't mind."

"Shut up." I twisted, face-planting in my pillow to hide my flaming cheeks. *Shit.*

The sound of his rich chuckle filled the room, and damn it, I liked that too.

It was his eyes that had been my downfall in high school. And his smile. He'd flashed those straight white teeth, locked me in with those crystal blue eyes, and before he'd even finished asking if I wanted to go on a second date, I'd said *yes, please.*

A zipper loosened. Denim rustled.

*Don't look. Don't look. Don't look.*

I cracked an eye, just in time to see Harrison bend, peeling off his jeans and his socks. Why couldn't he have a flat butt? Damn him.

That exquisite ass was only covered in a pair of white underwear.

The Harrison from my youth had been smoking hot. This version? He put teenaged Harrison to shame. A dull throb bloomed in my core, and with every second, it seemed to pulse harder.

I was supposed to share a bed with this man. Would he be able to feel me squirm? Would he hear my racing heart?

*No.* I stifled a groan.

Why did I have to be attracted to him? Why couldn't he be like Christopher or Matthew? They were each handsome, but to me, they'd always just be Harrison's buddies and the boys who'd cupped their hands in their armpits in junior high band practice to make fart noises.

Harrison stood tall, raking a hand through his dark hair before stretching an arm for the light. The movement show-cased the definition around his ribs, the dips and dents begging to be touched.

*No. No, no, no.* What was wrong with me? There would be *no* touching.

I snapped my eyes closed before he could catch me staring again, then scooted to the farthest edge of the bed as he killed the lights.

Harrison walked around the bed to his side, then pulled the covers back so hard they came loose from my shoulders. "Don't hog the quilt."

"I—" Before I could finish my protest, I clamped my mouth shut.

He was just trying to antagonize me. Well, I wasn't playing, not anymore. I'd ignore him for the rest of the night, then tomorrow, disappear before dawn.

He flopped in the bed, wrenching free the pillow I'd sandwiched between us. He kicked at the covers. He tugged at the sheets. The mattress bounced—and me with it—as he flipped from his back to his stomach. Until finally, he settled onto his side.

Except, unlike me, he wasn't facing the outside. I could feel his eyes on the back of my head. "Night, darlin'."

"Since you took away the pillow between us, know that if you so much as brush your foot against mine tonight, I will castrate you in your sleep."

"I have no desire to touch you, Anne." There wasn't a hint of teasing in his voice.

It stung. Why did that hurt?

Probably because he'd only wanted me for one thing in high school—my virginity—and now that he'd claimed it, I was no longer a prize.

*Asshole.*

I squeezed my eyes shut, ignoring his spicy, woody scent as it filled my nose. Harrison had always smelled good. That hadn't changed.

But he didn't want to touch me.

And I wasn't going to touch him.

I drew in a long breath, willing my mind to shut off. If I could just sleep for an hour or two, then I'd drive home. Except as our room quieted, a faint thud came from another.

*Thud. Thud. Thud.*

I pushed up on an elbow.

*Thud. Thud. Thud.*

A headboard was hitting the wall. Then came a moan.

"I hate my friends," I muttered.

"At least someone is having fun," Harrison said. "Want to have a go at it? For old time's sake?"

"You're a pig." I moved in a flash, sitting up and grabbing my pillow to slam in his face. It earned me a grumble as I flew out of the bed, yanking the quilt free from the mattress.

Screw it. I'd sleep on the damn floor.

"I'm just joking, Anne."

I flipped him off as I ripped open the door and stormed toward the living room.

Harrison's chuckle followed me all the way to the fireplace.

# CHAPTER FOUR

## HARRISON

The kink in my neck was going to last the rest of my life.

"Ugh," I groaned, pushing myself up to a seat on the floor. The blanket I'd slept under fell to my waist. The chill in the living room bit into my bare chest.

Beside me, there were only a few coals left in the fireplace, glowing orange in the black and gray ash.

I yawned, glancing toward the windows. It was still dark outside, but a faint light was beginning to creep through the trees.

My eyelids felt heavy. Every muscle in my body was stiff. I reached for my nape, massaging the ache at the base of my skull.

Last night, after Anne had stormed out of the bedroom, I'd listened to her rummage through cabinets and closets. She'd found a few extra blankets and had made herself a bed in front of the fireplace.

I'd waited until she'd fallen asleep on her makeshift bedroll before I'd gotten up and carried her to bed. She hadn't so much as stirred when I'd settled her on the bed. It had been easier that way. No angry glares. No snide comments. No arguments.

Knowing Anne, she might have insisted on sleeping on the floor just to prove a point.

Well, at least one of us had gotten some rest.

This floor was hard as hell, and the few blankets she found, I'd had to split, top to bottom. When I'd left the ranch yesterday, I'd thought about bringing my sleeping bag. Should have trusted my gut.

I cracked my neck, then rubbed my temples. It wasn't even dawn and I needed a nap.

The door to the bedroom creaked open from that noisy hinge.

Anne stood in the threshold, her dark hair wild and unruly as it draped over her shoulders. She was wearing a crimson-and-white-striped nightshirt that hit her midthigh. The sleeves cuffed at her wrists and the V-neck revealed a sliver of her collarbone. It wasn't all that sexy of a nightgown, but on Anne, it might as well have been lingerie.

Blood rushed to my groin, so I kept the blankets over my knees, wishing I would have snagged my jeans from the bedroom.

"You slept on the floor," she said, her voice quiet.

"Yep."

She dropped her gaze to her bare feet. "I was going to sleep out here."

"You did. For a while."

Anne looked up, her blue eyes locking with mine as she studied my face. "Why did you do that?"

"You really think I would have let you crash on the floor while I slept in the bed?" I scoffed. "Thought you knew me better than that."

"I thought I knew you once too."

Maybe we hadn't really known each other at all. The Anne I'd known would have at least given me a reason for ending it.

Last night, while I'd been cursing this goddamn floor, I'd replayed our relationship in high school. And just like six years ago, I'd come up short on answers.

This trip was ironically timed. Anne had broken up with me around New Year's Eve.

Six years, nearly to the day.

Maybe that was why I'd agreed to this trip. Because when Matthew had told me Anne was coming too, I'd wanted to see her. Maybe for the closure I hadn't gotten senior year.

Anne padded into the living room, wrapping her arms around her waist. Then she looked to the windows, seeing the snow piled up beyond the glass. "Brr. It's cold."

"Yeah." I shifted to my knees, adding a few pieces of kindling to the fire. Once it was ablaze, I added a log, listening to it pop and crackle.

Anne took a seat close to the hearth, joining me on the floor.

"Here." I took the blanket from my legs, standing to drape it over her shoulders before I went to the bedroom to pull on yesterday's jeans. Then I dug a fresh white T-shirt from my bag.

When I returned to the living room, Anne was holding her hands to the fire.

I came over and added another log, getting it nice and warm, then sunk back down to the space beside her.

Yeah, there were four chairs.

But it was warmer here.

The floor wasn't *that* bad.

"Thank you for the bed," she said, giving me a small smile.

That smile of hers was what had enchanted me my junior year in high school. I'd been standing at my locker, about to go to class, when she'd walked by. She'd flashed me that smile, shy and sweet, and I'd been a goner.

I'd known Anne since elementary school. She was two years younger, but Quincy was too small not to know every kid who roamed the halls. She'd always been cute. Pretty. I'd seen her smile countless times.

But something about that day by my locker, that particular smile, had lit a flame.

I'd missed that smile these six years.

"What if I would have stayed in the bed? Not come out here?" she asked.

"I was about a minute away from leaving the bed to you, but you beat me to it."

"Really?"

I shrugged. "I was just giving you a hard time."

"Why? Because I dumped you in high school? Was that my punishment?"

"Maybe." I grinned. "Or maybe I just like the way your cheeks turn red when you're mad."

She leveled me with a flat stare.

I chuckled. "How have you been?"

"Good. Ready to finish school."

"Yeah, I remember that feeling." By the time my senior year at Montana State had rolled around, I'd been more than ready to get the hell out of Bozeman and go back to Quincy. Go back to the ranch.

After I'd earned my bachelor's degree, I'd come home to

work. My brother, Briggs, didn't have much desire to take over the family businesses, but there hadn't been a time in my life when I hadn't wanted to step into my father's shoes.

So I'd worked for him these past two years. Listening. Learning.

"You're back on the ranch?" she asked.

"I am."

"That was always your dream."

"Still is." Grow old tending the land that had been in my family's name for generations. That was the dream. Maybe marry a beautiful woman along the way and build a legacy for our own children.

"I'm happy for you, Harrison."

"Liar."

She rolled her eyes. "I can be happy for you and also annoyed by you, all at the same time."

This woman. I laughed, shaking my head.

She'd changed. She'd grown bolder. Sassier. Part of me wished I would have been around for the past six years to witness that change myself.

"So . . . I slept on the floor."

"Don't expect my pity."

"Then how about an explanation? Why'd you break up with me?"

"You know why."

I held up a hand. "Swear to God, Anne. I don't."

She stared at me for a long moment, searching my gaze. "Really?"

"Tell me. Please." At that point in time, as a senior in high school, I'd known I was just months away from leaving, I hadn't made Anne any promises about the future. But I'd always treated her right, hadn't I?

"We went to dinner at the White Oak for New Year's Eve," she said.

"I remember."

I'd picked her up at her house, waved to her parents from my truck. Then we'd gone to dinner. But instead of me driving her home, her mom had come to pick her up. Probably because Anne and I had gotten busted the weekend before for making out outside their house.

She'd been acting strange all night. But every time I'd asked her if she was okay, she'd said yes. She'd just been quiet over our meal. I'd figured it had something to do with us getting caught and her being grounded all week.

The next day, I'd wanted to surprise her with a movie at the theater. So I'd gone to her house. But instead of starting off the New Year with a smile, she'd answered the door and told me never to speak to her again.

I'd been shocked. Pissed. Hurt.

That had been the first—and last—time anyone had slammed a door in my face.

"When my mom came to pick me up, you walked me to her car. Kissed me goodnight."

"Yeah." During dinner, I'd tried to convince her to sneak out of her bedroom window and meet me at midnight for a kiss, but she hadn't wanted to risk getting caught by her parents again. So we'd said happy New Year and she'd gone home.

"I forgot my scarf at the restaurant. Mom drove me back to get it, but she couldn't find a parking spot, so she dropped me at the end of the block. I was walking back and saw you standing by your truck, talking to David Johnson."

"Okay," I drawled. I didn't remember seeing her come

back. And I didn't remember what I'd been talking to David about.

"You were talking about *me*."

I blinked. Guess I had my answer.

What the hell had I said?

"He asked you when you were going to call it off," she told me. "And you said eventually."

"Well . . . I *was* leaving."

"David said you were hogging all of the good virgin pussy." Her teeth clenched. "And you said, *she's not a virgin anymore*."

I winced. *Damn.* "In my defense, it was true."

Anne smacked me on the shoulder. "Are you kidding me?"

"I'm sorry." I held up my hands. "I'm sorry. Look, David wanted you. Hell, all the guys wanted you. You were the prettiest girl in Quincy High and he was always chasing after the underclass girls."

"Eww." She cringed. "That's still not an excuse."

"You're right. I don't know why I said that. I don't know why I didn't punch him in the face." Because if a man talked about my woman like that now, yeah, he would have gotten punched. "I screwed up. That was none of his business, and I shouldn't have said a word. You deserved better than that."

My mother would have smacked me too if she'd heard this story.

"Oh." Anne's shoulders slumped, like maybe she'd been bracing herself for an argument.

I gave her a sideways glance. "That's it?"

She lifted a shoulder. "You forgot my birthday too."

"I did?" When the hell was her birthday?

"Yes. You were my boyfriend and you forgot my birthday."

Oops. High school Harrison hadn't won a lot of boyfriend awards. "Did you ever tell me when your birthday was?"

"We'd been dating for almost a year."

That wasn't really an answer, but there was an edge to her voice. An edge I'd heard last night. And I really didn't feel like fighting before I'd had some coffee.

"Well, uh, do you know my birthday?" I asked.

"April third."

"Oh." *Shit.* I hadn't expected an answer. Or that she'd remember after six years. "In my defense—"

Anne shot me a glare colder than the icicles hanging from the cabin's eaves.

"In my defense, I have never been good at stuff like that."

Her nostrils flared.

"Yeah, that excuse sounded a lot better in my head," I muttered. "How about another apology? Sorry."

The anger vanished from her expression, her shoulders slumping. "I was sixteen. I was convinced you were the love of my life. Then you forgot my birthday and told that creep David Johnson that you were going to dump me *eventually* and that I wasn't a virgin."

I'd deserved getting that door slammed in my face. "Yeah, I fucked up."

"Thank you." She sighed, turning to stare into the fire. The flames danced in her blue eyes and cast her face in gold.

I could have sat there for hours, staring at her profile, but coffee beckoned, so I stood and retreated to the kitchen to brew a pot.

Anne was still beside the fireplace on the floor when I returned with two steaming mugs.

"Happy birthday," I said.

Her face whipped to mine, her mouth parting. "How did you know?"

I handed her a cup, then used my free hand to dig her driver's license from my back pocket. "Stole this from your purse."

Maybe Amanda and Jessica knew it was her birthday and had brought supplies for a cake. Maybe a gift or two. They hadn't mentioned it yesterday, but I sure as hell hoped so.

"Took you long enough." Anne giggled, snatching her license from my hand.

And I refused to blink, not wanting to miss a second of her brilliant smile.

# CHAPTER FIVE

## ANNE

My lungs were on fire. My legs burned. Inside my coat and ski pants, my long underwear was sticking to my skin, and there was steam rising from my sweat-drenched head.

"Why are they going so fast?" I panted, staring down the trail ahead where Amanda, Jessica and their boyfriends were skiing across a meadow at a punishing pace.

For the first thirty minutes of this trek, I'd busted my ass to keep up. But I was seconds from puking my breakfast in the snow. If they went too much farther, there was a very good chance they'd have to carry me back to the cabin.

"You okay?" Harrison asked, glancing over his shoulder.

I dropped my hands to my knees, letting my poles dangle at my sides from the loops around my wrists. "You guys go ahead. I'll catch up." *Or not.*

He turned, stepping wide with his skis, and shuffled to my side.

"I hate cross-country skiing," I confessed, my breath

billowing as I dragged in breath after breath, attempting to calm my racing heart.

"Then why'd you come on a trip where cross-country skiing was the main event?"

"To torture myself?"

"On your birthday?"

I stood tall and shrugged a shoulder, seeing my friends get farther and farther ahead. Catching up was going to hurt. A lot. "I figured this would be a nice, leisurely outing. Not a marathon."

Harrison chuckled. "These guys go out almost every weekend. It's not easy keeping up."

"You don't seem to be having any trouble," I muttered.

His cheeks were flushed but more from the cold than exertion. He wasn't out of breath or sweating buckets. No, he looked perfect on this wintry day, wearing a black snowsuit with a narrow band of yellow on the sides. His black, wool scotch cap had a brim that shielded his eyes from the sun.

"Do you want to turn back?" he asked.

I opened my mouth to say no, that we'd catch the group and I'd survive, but a fresh wave of exhaustion crashed through my bones. "Yes," I admitted.

He twisted, sending out a piercing whistle through the winter air.

Our friends stopped, looking back.

"We're heading back!" he called.

Christopher raised a ski pole in the air, signaling he'd heard the message.

"You don't have to come with me," I said. "You can keep going."

"I don't mind," he said. "I won't make you suffer alone on your birthday."

It was about the tenth time he'd brought up my birthday, like now that he knew the date, he was determined never to forget again.

Amanda and Jessica had remembered and brought along the ingredients to make a cake later. Amanda had knitted me a new stocking hat—currently on my sweaty head. And Jessica had given me two new books—the latest Stephen King novel and *The Shell Seekers* by Rosamunde Pilcher which had just come out and I'd been wanting to read.

The gifts and cake were special. But it was Harrison's attention that had been the most flattering today. At breakfast, every time I'd looked his direction, his eyes had been waiting.

He'd seemed genuinely sorry this morning when we'd talked about the past. Maybe this attention of his was his way to make amends.

And maybe I'd been a tad dramatic. To steal his phrase . . .

In my defense, what sixteen-year-old girl wasn't dramatic?

Mostly, I was just glad we'd cleared the air. Now the next time I bumped into him in Quincy, it wouldn't be awkward.

"When do you head back to school?" he asked, both of us falling into a gentle glide with our skis, shuffling left, then right, then left again.

"Tomorrow. I'll go home, pack up my stuff, then head to Missoula. Classes start again on Monday."

"What are you studying?"

"Business."

"Do you like it?"

I shrugged. "It's all right. I like school. Some classes are more challenging than others."

"And what will you do after graduation?"

"No hard questions on my birthday, please."

He smiled, his eyes twinkling.

God, he really was something, wasn't he? It was hard to look away, but I forced my gaze to the view.

This was a beautiful spot. The meadow was hugged by towering evergreens, their bows dusted in white from last night's storm. The snow was fluffy, blanketing the ground and sparkling beneath the sun. But the scenery paled in comparison to the man at my side.

Probably a good thing I was leaving tomorrow. Before I did something stupid, like kiss that sinful mouth.

I'd debated heading out this morning, following through on my plan from last night. But Amanda and Jessica had been so excited that I was here for my birthday—and that Harrison and I were no longer at each other's throats—so I'd stayed.

At the moment, even sweaty and tired, I had no regrets.

"I'm not sure what I want to do after graduation," I told him.

"Will you stay in Missoula?"

"Maybe. I like my job. I work as a bookkeeper for a small hotel. The owners are this lovely couple. They're very kind, albeit a bit unorganized. Which is the reason why I'm there. But it's not my dream job. I don't know if I have a dream job."

"You'll find it."

"Possibly. But I'm oddly okay if I don't." I didn't need grand accomplishments or accolades for my achievements. I was happily content to simply be . . . happily content.

"Would you ever move back home to Quincy?" he asked.

"Yes. If I could find a job, I'd move home." Over Christmas, I'd browsed the classifieds for job postings. There wasn't much open at the moment, but I'd keep looking.

Quincy was home. Being closer to my family, my friends, would be nice. Sure, I had friends in Missoula, but after graduation, most would be leaving for jobs. The only person staying was the tape thief Jeremy. It would be worth moving just so I wouldn't have to risk seeing his face ever again.

"So what do you want to do when we get back to the cabin, Birthday Girl?" Harrison asked as we approached a cluster of trees.

"Take a shower. A long, hot shower."

"I like long, hot showers." Innuendo dripped from his tone.

The image of us together, me wrapped around his strong, muscled body, flashed in my mind. A pulse bloomed in my core. Thankfully, my face was already flushed or he'd know exactly what I'd been thinking.

I risked a glance at his profile, taking in the soft pout of his lips. Would he taste the same as he had when we'd been younger?

Harrison had been my first everything. He'd taught me about pleasure. About letting go of my inhibitions. About taking what I desired. That had been a powerful lesson for a sixteen-year-old young woman. He'd set the bar for any future lovers, and thus far, they'd all failed spectacularly.

What would it be like after all this time? Worse? Better?

Why was I even curious? Harrison and I had just barely patched up a—what were we? No longer enemies. But were we friends? Well, we weren't lovers. So why was I thinking about sex?

I pushed my legs harder, picking up the pace to get back to the cabin. As soon as we arrived, I stripped off my skis, leaving them in the bed of my truck, then went inside and locked myself in the bathroom, needing a few moments away from Harrison to sort out my head.

A lukewarm shower should have helped, except the tepid water did nothing to cool the fire in my veins, and when I opened the bedroom door, my hair combed but wet, I found Harrison crouched beside the fireplace, his snow gear gone and a beer in hand.

"Want one?" He raised the bottle.

"Um, sure. I can get it." I walked to the kitchen, taking a beer from the fridge. I gulped half of it before going to the living room, taking the chair as far away from him as possible.

"Think I'll take a shower too. Would you mind?" He pointed to the bedroom. My bedroom. Where there was a bed. A cozy bed. And soon to be a very naked Harrison.

*Gah!* "No, um, go for it."

"You okay?"

"Great," I said, too brightly.

"Sorry I don't have a birthday gift for you."

"It's fine. It's not like you knew it was today." I waved it off. Though I could think of one gift he could give me.

An orgasm.

My cheeks flamed.

He studied my face, his Adam's apple bobbing, like he could read my thoughts. Then he swallowed hard before clearing his throat, giving a slight headshake as he walked out of the living room.

Except instead of disappearing into the bedroom, he paused outside the threshold, glancing back. "Anne . . ."

"What?" I breathed.

"It's, uh . . . nothing." He did another headshake. "Never mind."

I held my breath, waiting for him to retreat into the bedroom. But he stood there, his eyes aimed at an invisible spot between us. His shoulders and arms were tense, the muscles bulging beneath his T-shirt.

My gaze raked down his spine, to the curve of his ass in those jeans, the leather Wrangler patch on a back pocket.

The throb in my core vibrated through my entire body.

Oh, how I wanted Harrison Eden.

But I didn't move from the chair. I waited, watching, as he stood rooted to that spot.

He dragged a hand through his dark hair, making it stick up at odd angles. Then he took a step for the bedroom.

The air rushed from my lungs. Was it relief? Or disappointment?

*Disappointment.* Definitely disappointment.

Maybe he could sense it from across the room. Maybe he was just as weak as I was. Because one moment he was heading for the shower, then the next, he was stalking my way.

"Fuck it." He strode across the living room, straight to my chair. His hands delved into my hair, the calluses on his fingers brushing my cheeks.

Then he sealed his mouth over mine.

And Harrison tasted better than I'd remembered.

# CHAPTER SIX

## HARRISON

Fuck, but Anne tasted sweet.

I slid my tongue against hers in a lazy swirl, earning a quiet moan. Fire blazed through my veins, and the urge to strip her out of those clothes was almost crippling. My control was dangling by a thread, so before I pushed too far, I tore my mouth away, locking my gaze with hers. "Tell me to stop."

She shoved out of the chair, standing on her toes to whisper against my lips, "Don't stop."

*Thank fuck.* I swept her into my arms, slanting my mouth over hers, my tongue delving into every corner, savoring that sweet taste.

Anne's hands came to my chest, her palms dragging over the cotton of my shirt, up my pecs, then down my stomach, attempting to get to the fly on my jeans but I held her too close.

I wanted to taste her, memorize this mouth, before I moved on to other parts of her body.

I'd told her earlier that I'd fucked up. Yeah. Not fighting harder for her six years ago had been a major fuckup. A mistake I'd fix today.

She matched my intensity, beat for beat, kissing me with the same desperation, like she'd forgotten just how good we'd been together.

It was good. So damn good. Better than I remembered.

My teeth nipped at the corner of her mouth. My hands drifted to cup her ass and squeeze. My tongue fluttered against hers, a move that won me a whimper and tiny smile.

She'd always liked that flutter, especially between her legs.

"Bedroom," I breathed against her lips, barely breaking the kiss.

We shuffled together, our mouths fused, until we were past the door enough I could kick it closed. Then I spun her around, keeping my arms banded tight, as I laid us on the bed.

Her long legs spread wide, her hips cradling mine as I pressed my arousal against her core. Anne's breath hitched as I rocked my cock against her center, the denim of our jeans adding a bit of friction but it wasn't enough. I needed more. I needed skin and her tight heat.

So I lifted the hem of her tee, dragging it up her stomach. Then I freed a breast from her bra, pulling the cup down to latch my mouth over a nipple, sucking hard.

"Harrison." She hissed, reaching for the hem of my T-shirt, attempting to tug it free.

I let go of her nipple with a *pop*, then reached behind my neck to yank my shirt over my head. "How far do you want to take this? No regrets." If she just wanted to fool around, kiss and rub on each other, I'd quit whenever she said enough. But if she wanted an orgasm or two, I'd gladly be the man who delivered.

Her eyes softened. "You used to ask me that."

"Huh?"

"Before we had sex, you always used to ask me how far." Her fingertips touched the hair by my temple. "I like that you have changed. But that you also . . . haven't."

I kissed the corner of her mouth, then dipped lower to drag my tongue over her bared nipple. Her breasts were fuller than they'd been in high school. Her skin softer. Her moans more melodic. "I want to taste every inch of this body."

"Yes." She arched into my mouth. "I want it all. I want you."

My chest tightened as I lifted, drowning in her eyes. God, she was stunning. So perfect it was hard to breathe.

Something was happening here, something that felt a lot like the future. Something too serious to get hung up on at the moment.

So I shoved those feelings away and stood off the bed, reaching behind her knees to drag her ass to the edge of the mattress. Then I plucked the button free on her jeans, loosening the zipper and stripping the pants from her legs. They landed with a plop as I hauled off her panties, tossing them over my shoulder.

"Damn, you are perfect." I dropped to my knees, peppering a trail of kisses along the inside of her thigh.

Anne's entire body trembled. "Harrison."

Another day, another night, I'd torture her a bit. Tease her until she begged for my mouth. But today, I was too desperate, so I flattened my tongue and dragged it through her glistening folds.

"Oh, God," she cried, slapping a hand over her mouth.

I didn't give a shit if everyone else returned from skiing and heard us. One taste of Anne's pussy, and I'd shout from the mountaintops that it was mine.

Her hands came to my hair, threading through the longer strands on top, holding me to her as I licked again. Then I fluttered my tongue through her slit. "Fuck, darlin'. You taste so good."

She hummed as I lapped at her.

"You missed my tongue, didn't you?"

"Yes," she murmured, her grip on my hair tightening.

I reached for her other breast, yanking the cup of her bra free to roll her nipple between my thumb and finger, all while I fucked her with my tongue.

Every day. I would feast on this woman every day if she'd let me.

"Harrison." She rocked her hips, riding my face. "I want you inside."

Not a chance. First, I wanted her to come on my face.

Her legs began to shake, so I took her knees, spreading them wide and holding them apart. Then I latched on to her clit and sucked. Hard.

Anne's back arched off the bed, her cry echoed through the room.

I fluttered my tongue again, alternating between licking and sucking, until her entire body was shaking. Then I backed off, straightening just enough to see the ecstasy on her face. "Your pussy is so sweet."

"Don't stop." Her chest heaved, her eyes wild. "Please."

I grinned, then dropped again, taking her in my mouth. And this time, I didn't stop. I added a finger, sliding in to stroke her inner walls as I sucked on her clit. With the other hand, I held her leg, pinning it down until her muscles tensed, her heels digging into the edge of the bed and her toes curling.

"I'm—" That was the only warning before she exploded on a cry, coming on my tongue and clenching around my finger.

I kept at her, not letting up until the pulsing ebbed. When her body finally sagged into the bed, I stood, digging into a pocket for my wallet. I fished out a condom, unzipping my jeans and shoving them to the floor. Then when I was covered, I lifted a breathless Anne deeper into the bed.

She cracked her eyes open, giving me a sexy smile as she spread her legs again, making room for my hips. "I don't remember your tongue being that talented."

"My tongue always loved you." I reached between us to fist my shaft and drag the tip through her soaked center. "My cock did too. Let's see if that's the same."

Anne opened her mouth, probably to throw some sass my way, but I thrust deep, stealing her breath.

"Fuck." I gritted my teeth, summoning every ounce of restraint not to come. Goddamn, she was tight. She fit me like a glove.

"Oh, God." Her hands came to my shoulders, her nails digging into my flesh as she stretched around me. "Move."

I leaned in, latching my mouth on to her neck, then eased out before slamming in again, earning another cry from those pretty lips.

"I forgot." Her voice was so quiet I could barely make out

the words. Maybe I would have missed them, except I'd been thinking the same damn thing.

*I forgot.*

I'd forgotten just how good we'd been together. Even as fumbling teenagers, learning about each other, we'd been good.

But this . . .

No contest.

Anne clung to me as I brought us together, thrust after thrust, until she writhed beneath me and the pressure at the base of my spine neared its peak. She pulled her bottom lip between her teeth, gasped, then detonated.

"Oh, fuck," I growled, her orgasm triggering mine.

White spots broke across my vision, a roar came from deep in my chest, totally unrestrained and raw. My limbs were shaking as the release slammed into me like a tidal wave, hit after hit, until I was boneless and collapsed into Anne's arms.

She wrapped me tight, her legs winding around my hips.

Our heartbeats thundered. Our breaths ragged. Our skin sticky with sweat.

"Wow." She exhaled, then laughed.

How did you go six years missing a laugh and not even realize it?

"Darlin'." I rolled to my back and took her with me, hauling her onto my chest. "We're screwed."

"What do you mean?" She sat up, her eyes narrowing as she tucked a lock of hair behind an ear.

My hand drifted to her bare ass. "Six or seven?"

Anne blinked. "Six or seven, what?"

"Kids."

She sat up even straighter, forcing us to break our connection. "Wait. What? We're not having kids. We used a condom."

"We're not having kids today. But eventually I'd like kids. Don't you?"

Anne opened her mouth. Closed it. Opened it again.

I shoved up on an elbow, grinning as I pushed more of her hair from her face. "You said you didn't have plans after college."

"I wasn't looking for you to solve that problem for me."

"You're going back to Missoula tomorrow," I said, more to myself than her. Maybe I could get away from the ranch in a few days. Maybe Thursday if I could get one of the hands to cover. Most likely, it would be Friday. But there was no way I was going longer than a week without her.

"Yes," she said. "And you're going home to Quincy."

"I'll come see you next weekend."

"Harrison—"

"This is good. Real good. Have you ever had it better?"

She sighed. "No."

"We gotta give this a chance."

"You're talking about children. That's more than a chance."

"If it all works out, then yeah. Why not? You'll finish up school. Come home to Quincy. We'll get married. Have a hell of a time making seven kids."

She did that open, close, open thing with her mouth again. "Are you insane?"

Damn, it was going to be fun teasing her for the next fifty years.

"You're right." I rubbed my jaw, fighting a smile. "Seven is too many. We'll just have six."

———

Want to meet those six kids of Anne and Harrison's? The Edens is a series of six, standalone small-town, contemporary romances, starting with Indigo Ridge. Turn the page to read a preview.

# PREVIEW TO INDIGO RIDGE

Enjoy this preview from Indigo Ridge, book one in The Edens series.

WINSLOW

"Could I get another . . ."

The bartender didn't slow as he passed by.

"Drink," I muttered, slumping forward.

Pops had told me that this bar was where the locals hung out. Not only was it within walking distance of my new house in case I decided not to drive, but I was a local now. As of today, I lived in Quincy, Montana.

I'd told the bartender as much when I'd asked for his wine list. He'd raised one bushy white eyebrow above his narrowed gaze, and I'd abandoned my thirst for a glass of cabernet, ordering a vodka tonic instead. It had zapped every ounce of my willpower not to request a lemon twist.

The ice cubes in my glass clinked together as I swirled

around my pink plastic straw. The bartender ignored that sound too.

Main Street had two bars—tourist traps this time of year, according to Pops. But I regretted not choosing one of those to celebrate my first night in Quincy. Given his attitude, the bartender, who must have thought I was a lost tourist, regretted my decision too.

Willie's was a dive bar and not exactly my scene.

The bartenders downtown probably acknowledged their customers, and the prices were listed on a menu, not delivered using three fingers on one wrinkled hand.

He looked about as old as this dark, dingy building. Like most small-town Montana bars, the walls were teeming with beer signs and neon lights. Shelves stacked with liquor bottles lined the mirrored wall across from my seat. The room was cluttered with tables, every chair empty.

Willie's was all but deserted this Sunday night at nine o'clock.

The locals must know of a better place to unwind.

The only other patron was a man sitting at the farthest end of the bar, in the last stool down the line. He'd come in ten minutes after I'd arrived and chosen the seat as far from me as possible. He and the bartender were nearly carbon copies of one another, with the same white hair and scraggly beards.

Twins? They looked old enough to have established this bar. Maybe one of them was Willie himself.

The bartender caught me staring.

I smiled and rattled the ice in my glass.

His mouth pursed in a thin line but he made me another drink. And like with the first, he delivered it without a word, holding up the same three fingers.

I twisted to reach into my purse, fishing out another five because clearly starting a tab was out of the question. But before I could pull the bill from my wallet, a deep, rugged voice caressed the room.

"Hey, Willie."

"Griffin." The bartender nodded.

So he was Willie. And he could speak.

"Usual?" Willie asked.

"Yep." The man with the incredible voice, Griffin, pulled out the stool two down from mine.

As his tall, broad body eased into the seat, a whiff of his scent carried my way. Leather and wind and spice filled my nose, chasing away the musty air from the bar. It was heady and alluring.

He was the type of man who turned a woman's head.

One glimpse at his profile and the cocktail in front of me was unnecessary. Instead, I drank this man in head to toe.

The sleeves of his black T-shirt stretched around his honed biceps and molded to the planes of his shoulders as he leaned his elbows on the bar. His brown hair was finger-combed and curled at the nape of his neck. His tan forearms were dusted with the same dark hair and a vein ran over the corded muscle beneath.

Even seated, I could tell his legs were long, his thighs thick like the evergreen tree trunks from the forests outside of town. Frayed hems of his faded jeans brushed against his black cowboy boots. And as he shifted in his seat, I caught the glimmer of a silver and gold belt buckle at his waist.

If his voice, his scent and that chiseled jaw hadn't been enough to make my mouth go dry, that buckle would have done it.

One of my mom's favorite movies had been *Legends of*

*the Fall*. She'd let me watch it at sixteen and we'd cried together. Whenever I missed her, I'd put it on. The DVD was scratched and the clasp on the case was broken because I'd watched that movie countless times simply because it had been hers.

She'd always swooned over Brad Pitt as a sexy cowboy.

If she could see Griffin, she'd be drooling too. Though he was missing the hat and the horse, this guy was every cowboy fantasy come to life.

Lifting my glass to my mouth, I sipped the cold drink and tore my gaze from the handsome stranger. The vodka burned my throat and the alcohol rushed to my head. Ol' Willie mixed his cocktails strong.

I was unabashedly staring. It was rude and obvious. Yet when I set the glass down, my gaze immediately returned to Griffin.

His piercing blue eyes were waiting.

My breath hitched.

Willie set down a tumbler full of ice and caramel liquid in front of Griffin, then, without giving him the fingers to pay, walked away.

Griffin took a single swallow of his drink, his Adam's apple bobbing. Then his attention was on me once more.

The intensity of his gaze was as intoxicating as my cocktail.

He stared without hesitation. He stared with bold desire. His gaze raked down my black tank top to the ripped jeans I'd put on this morning before checking out of my hotel in Bozeman.

I'd spent four and a half hours driving to Quincy with a U-Haul trailer hitched to my Dodge Durango. When I'd arrived, I'd immediately jumped into unloading, only breaking to meet Pops for dinner.

I was a mess after a day of hauling boxes. My hair was in a ponytail and whatever makeup I'd put on this morning had likely worn off. Yet the appreciation in Griffin's gaze sent a wave of desire rushing to my core.

"Hi," I blurted. *Smooth, Winn.*

His eyes twinkled like two perfect sapphires set behind long, sooty lashes. "Hi."

"I'm Winn." I held out a hand over the space between us.

"Griffin." The moment his warm, calloused palm grazed mine, tingles cascaded across my skin like fireworks. A shiver rolled down my spine.

Holy hell. There was enough electricity between us to power the jukebox in the corner.

I focused on my drink, gulping more than sipping. The ice did nothing to cool me down. When was the last time I'd been this attracted to a man? Years. It had been years. Even then, it paled in comparison to five minutes beside Griffin.

"Where are you from?" he asked. Like Willie, he must have assumed I was a tourist too.

"Bozeman."

He nodded. "I went to college at Montana State."

"Go Bobcats." I lifted my drink in a salute.

Griffin returned the gesture, then put the rim of his glass to his full lower lip.

I was staring again, unashamed. Maybe it was the angular cheekbones that set his face apart. Maybe it was the straight nose with a slight bump at the bridge. Or his dark, bold browbone. He was no ordinary, handsome man. Griffin was drop-dead gorgeous.

And if he was at Willie's . . . a local.

Local meant off-limits. *Damn.*

I swallowed my disappointment with another gulp of vodka.

The scrape of stool legs rang through the room as he moved to take the seat beside mine. His arms returned to the bar, his drink between them as he leaned forward. He sat so close, his body so large, that the heat from his skin seeped into mine.

"Winn. I like that name."

"Thanks." My full name was Winslow but very few people ever called me anything other than Winn or Winnie.

Willie walked by and narrowed his eyes at the sliver of space between Griffin and me. Then he joined his doppelganger.

"Are they related?" I asked, dropping my voice.

"Willie Senior is on our side of the bar. His son is mixing drinks."

"Father and son. Huh. I thought twins. Does Willie Senior have the same glowing personality as Willie Junior?"

"It's worse." Griffin chuckled. "Every time I come through town, he gets crankier."

Wait. Did that mean . . . "You don't live in town?"

"No." He shook his head, picking up his drink.

I did the same, hiding my smile in the glass. So he wasn't a local. Which meant flirting was harmless. *Bless you, Quincy.*

A hundred personal questions raced through my mind, but I dismissed them all. Skyler used to criticize me for going into interrogation mode within ten minutes of meeting someone new. One of many critiques. He'd used his profession as a life coach as an excuse to tell me anything and everything I'd been doing wrong in our relationship. In life.

Meanwhile, he'd betrayed me, so I wasn't listening to Skyler's voice anymore.

But I still wasn't going to bombard this man with questions. He didn't live here, and I'd save my questions for the people who did: my constituents.

Griffin looked to the far end of the room and the empty shuffleboard table. "Want to play a game?"

"Um . . . sure? I've never played before."

"It's easy." He slid off his stool, moving with a grace that men his size didn't normally possess.

I followed, eyes glued to the best ass I had ever seen. And he didn't live here. An imaginary choir perched in the bar's dusty rafters gave a collective *yeehaw*.

Griffin went to one end of the table while I walked to the other. "Okay, Winn. Loser buys the next round of drinks."

Good thing I had cash. "Okay."

Griffin spent the next ten minutes explaining the rules and demonstrating how to slide the pucks down the sand-dusted surface toward the point lines. Then we played, game after game. After one more round, we both stopped drinking, but neither of us made a move to leave.

I won some games. I lost most. And when Willie finally announced that he was closing at one, the two of us walked outside to the darkened parking lot.

A dusty black truck was parked beside my Durango.

"That was fun."

"It was." I smiled up at Griffin, my cheeks pinching. I hadn't had this much fun openly flirting with a man in, well . . . ever. I slowed my steps because the last place I wanted to go was home alone.

He must have had the same idea because his boots stopped on the pavement. He inched closer.

Winslow Covington didn't have one-night stands. I'd been too busy wasting years on the wrong man. Griffin wasn't the right man either, but I'd learned in my time as a cop that sometimes it wasn't about choosing right from wrong. It was choosing the *right* wrongs.

Griffin. Tonight, I chose Griffin.

So I closed the distance between us and stood on my toes, letting my hands snake up his hard, flat stomach.

He was tall, standing two or three inches over six feet. At five nine, it was refreshing to be around a man who towered over me. I lifted a hand to his neck, pulling him down until his mouth hovered over mine.

"Is that your truck?"

---

"Shit." I cursed at the clock, then flew into action, flinging the covers off my naked body and racing for the bathroom.

Late was not how I wanted to start the first day of my new job.

I flipped on the shower, my head pounding as I stepped under the cold spray and let out a yelp. There was no time to wait for hot water, so I shampooed my hair and put in some conditioner while I scrubbed Griffin's scent off my skin. I'd mourn the loss of it later.

There was an ache between my legs that I'd think about later too. Last night had been . . .

Mind blowing. Toe curling. The best night I'd ever had with a man. Griffin knew exactly how to use that powerful body of his and I'd been the lucky recipient of three—or had it been four?—orgasms.

I shuddered and realized the water was hot. "Damn it."

Shoving thoughts of Griffin out of my head, I hurried out of the shower, frantically swiping on makeup and willing the blow dryer to work faster. Without time to curl or straighten my hair, I twisted it into a tight bun at the nape of my neck, then dashed to the bedroom to get dressed.

The mattress rested on the floor, the sheets and blankets rumpled and strewn everywhere. Thankfully, before I'd headed to the bar last night, I'd searched for bedding in the boxes and laid it out. When I'd finally gotten home after hours spent in the back of Griffin's truck, I'd practically face-planted into my pillows and forgotten to set my alarm.

I refused to regret Griffin. Kicking off my new life in Quincy with a hot and wild night seemed a little bit like fate.

Serendipity.

Maybe on his next trip through town, we'd bump into each other. But if not, well . . . I didn't have time for the distraction of a man.

Especially not today.

"Oh, God. Please don't let me be late." I rifled through a suitcase, finding a pair of dark-wash jeans.

Pops had told me specifically not to show up at the station looking fancy.

The jeans were slightly wrinkled but there was no time to find whatever box had stolen my iron. Besides, an iron meant fancy. The simple white tee I found next was also wrinkled, so I dug for my favorite black blazer to hide the worst offenders. Then I hopped into my favorite black boots with the chunky heels before jogging for the door, swiping up my purse from where I'd dumped it on the living room floor.

The sun was shining. The air was clean. The sky was blue. And I had no time to appreciate a minute of my first

Quincy, Montana, morning as I ran to the Durango parked in my driveway.

I slid behind the wheel, started the engine and cursed again at the clock on the dash. *Eight-oh-two.* "I'm late."

Thankfully, Quincy wasn't Bozeman and the drive from one side of town to the police station on the other took exactly six minutes. I pulled into the lot and parked next to a familiar blue Bronco and let myself take a single deep breath.

*I can do this job.*

Then I got out of my car and walked to the station's front door, hoping with every step I looked okay.

One disdaining look from the officer stationed behind a glass partition at the front desk and I knew I'd gotten it wrong. *Shit.*

His gray hair was cut short, high and tight in a military style. He looked me up and down, the wrinkles on his face deepening with a scowl. That glare likely had nothing to do with my outfit.

And everything to do with my last name.

"Good morning." I plastered on a bright smile, crossing the small lobby to his workspace. "I'm Winslow Covington."

"The new chief. I know," he muttered.

My smile didn't falter.

I'd win them over. Eventually. That's what I'd told Pops last night when he'd had me over for dinner after I'd returned the U-Haul. I'd win them all over, one by one.

Most people were bound to think that the only reason I'd gotten the job as the Quincy chief of police was because my grandfather was the mayor. Yes, he would be my boss. But there wasn't a nepotism clause for city employees. Probably because in a town this size, everyone was likely related in some manner. If you added too many restrictions, no one would be able to get a job.

Besides, Pops hadn't hired me. He could have, but instead, he'd put together a search committee so that there'd be more than one voice in the decision. Walter Covington was the fairest, most honorable man I'd ever known.

And granddaughter or not, what mattered was my performance. He'd take the cues from the community, and though my grandfather loved me completely, he wouldn't hesitate to fire me if I screwed this up.

He'd told me as much the day he'd hired me. He'd reminded me again last night.

"The mayor is waiting in your office," the officer said, pushing the button to buzz me into the door beside his cubicle.

"It was nice to meet you"—I glanced at the silver name-plate on his black uniform—"Officer Smith."

His response was to ignore me completely, turning his attention to his computer screen. I'd have to win him over another day. Or maybe he'd be open to an early retirement.

I pushed through the door that led into the heart of the station. I'd been here twice, both times during the interview process. But it was different now as I walked through the bullpen no longer a guest. This was my bullpen. The officers looking up from their desks were under my charge.

My stomach clenched.

Staying up all night having sex with a stranger probably hadn't been the smartest way to prepare for my first day.

"Winnie." Pops came out of what would be my office, his hand extended. He seemed taller today, probably because he was dressed in nice jeans and a starched shirt instead of the

61

ratty T-shirt, baggy jeans and suspenders I'd seen him in yesterday.

Pops was fit for his seventy-one years and though his hair was a thick silver, his six-three frame was as strong as an ox. He was in better shape than most men my age, let alone his.

I shook his hand, glad that he hadn't tried to hug me. "Morning. Sorry I'm late."

"I just got here myself." He leaned in closer and dropped his voice. "You doing okay?"

"Nervous," I whispered.

He gave me a small smile. "You'll do great."

I could do this job.

I was thirty years old. Two decades below the median age of a person in this position. Four decades younger than my predecessor had been when he'd retired.

The former chief of police had worked in Quincy for his entire career, moving up the ranks and acting as chief for as long as I'd been alive. But that was why Pops had wanted me in this position. He said Quincy needed fresh eyes and younger blood. The town was growing, and with it, their problems. The old ways weren't cutting it.

The department needed to embrace technology and new processes. When the former chief had announced his retirement, Pops had encouraged me to toss my name into the hat. By some miracle, the hiring committee had chosen me.

Yes, I was young, but I met the minimum qualifications. I'd worked for ten years with the Bozeman Police Department. During that time, I'd earned my bachelor's degree and a position as detective within their department. My record was impeccable, and I'd never left a case unclosed.

Maybe my welcome would have been warmer if I were a

man, but that had never scared me and it certainly wasn't going to today.

*I can do this job.*

I would do this job.

"Let me introduce you to Janice." He nodded for me to follow him into my office, where we spent the morning with Janice, my new assistant.

She'd worked for the former chief for fifteen years, and the longer she spoke, the more I fell in love with her. Janice had spiky gray hair and the cutest pair of red-framed glasses I'd ever seen. She knew the ins and outs of the station, the schedules and the shortcomings.

As we ended our initial meeting, I made a mental note to bring her flowers because without Janice, I'd likely fall flat on my face. We toured the station, meeting the officers not out on patrol.

Officer Smith, who was rarely sent into the field because he preferred the desk, had been one of the candidates for chief, and Janice told me that he'd been a grumpy asshole since the day he'd been rejected.

Every officer besides him had been polite and professional, though reserved. No doubt they weren't sure what to make of me, but today I'd won Janice over—or maybe she'd won me. I was calling it a victory.

"You'll meet most of the department this afternoon at shift change," she told me when we retreated back to the safety of my office.

"I was planning on staying late one evening this week to meet the night shift too."

This wasn't a large station, because Quincy wasn't a large town, but in total, I had fifteen officers, four dispatchers, two administrators and a Janice.

"Tomorrow, the county sheriff is coming in to meet you," Janice said, reading from the notebook she'd had with her all morning. "Ten o'clock. His staff is twice the size of ours but he has more ground to cover. For the most part, their team stays out of our way, but he's always willing to step in if you need help."

"Good to know." I wouldn't mind having a resource to bounce ideas off of either.

"How's your head?" Pops asked.

I put my hands by my ears and made the sound of an exploding bomb.

He laughed. "You'll catch on."

"Yes, you will," Janice said.

"Thank you for everything," I told her. "I'm really looking forward to working with you."

She sat a little straighter. "Likewise."

"Okay, Winnie." Pops slapped his hands on his knees. "Let's go grab some lunch. Then I've got to get to my own office, and I'll let you come back here and settle in."

"I'll be here when you get back." Janice squeezed my arm as we shuffled out of my office.

Pops simply nodded, maintaining his distance. Tonight, when I wasn't Chief Covington and he wasn't Mayor Covington, I'd head to his house and get one of his bear hugs.

"How about we eat at The Eloise?" he suggested as we made our way outside.

"The hotel?"

He nodded. "It would be good for you to spend some time there. Get to know the Edens."

The Edens. Quincy's founding family.

Pops had promised that the fastest way to earn favor with the community was to win over the Edens. One of their relatives from generations past had founded the town and the family had been the community's cornerstone ever since.

"They own the hotel, remember?" he asked.

"I remember. I just didn't realize there was a restaurant in the hotel these days." Probably because I hadn't spent much time in Quincy lately.

The six trips I'd taken here to participate in the interview process had been my first trips to Quincy in years. Five, to be exact.

But when Skyler and I had fallen to pieces and Pops had pitched the job as chief, I'd decided it was time for a change. And Quincy, well . . . Quincy had always held a special place in my heart.

"The Edens started the hotel's restaurant about four years ago," Pops said. "It's the best place in town, in my opinion."

"Then let's eat." I unlocked my car. "Meet you there."

I followed his Bronco from the station to Main Street, taking in the plethora of out-of-state cars parked downtown. Tourist season was in full swing and nearly every space was full.

Pops parked two blocks away from Main on a side street, and side by side, we strolled to The Eloise Inn.

The town's iconic hotel was the tallest building in Quincy, standing proudly against the mountain backdrop in the distance. I'd always wanted to spend a night at The Eloise. Maybe one day I'd book myself a room, just for fun.

The lobby smelled of lemons and rosemary. The front desk was an island in the grand, open space, and a young woman with a sweet face stood behind the counter, checking in a guest. When she spotted Pops, she tossed him a wink.

"Who's that?" I asked.

"Eloise Eden. She took over as manager this past winter."

Pops waved at her, then walked past the front desk toward an open doorway. The clatter of forks on plates and the dull murmur of conversation greeted me as we entered the hotel's restaurant.

The dining room was spacious and the ceilings as tall as those in the lobby. It was the perfect place for entertaining. Almost a ballroom but filled with tables of varying sizes, it also worked well as a restaurant.

"They just put in those windows." Pops pointed at the far wall where black-paned windows cut into a red-brick wall. "Last time I talked to Harrison, he said this fall they'll be remodeling this whole space."

Harrison Eden. The family's patriarch. He'd been on the hiring committee, and I liked to believe I'd made a good impression. According to Pops, if I hadn't, there was no way I'd have gotten my job.

A hostess greeted us with a wide smile and led us to a square table in the center of the room.

"Which of the Edens runs the restaurant?" I asked as we browsed the menu card.

"Knox. He's Harrison and Anne's second oldest son. Eloise is their youngest daughter."

Harrison and Anne, the parents. Knox, a son. Eloise, a daughter. There were likely many more Edens to meet.

Down Main, the Eden name was splashed on numerous storefronts, including the coffee shop I wished I'd had time to stop by this morning. Last night's antics were catching up to me, and I hid a yawn with my menu.

"They're good people," Pops said. "You've met Harrison. Anne's a sweetheart. Their opinion carries a lot of weight around here. So does Griffin's."

Griffin. *Did he say Griffin?*

My stomach dropped.

No. This couldn't be happening. It had to be a mistake. There had to be another Griffin, one who didn't live in Quincy. I'd specifically asked him last night if he lived in town and he'd said no. Hadn't he?

"Hey, Covie."

So busy having my mental freak-out that I'd slept with not only a local man, but one I needed to see me as a professional and not a backseat hookup, I didn't notice the two men standing beside our table until it was too late.

Harrison Eden smiled.

Griffin, who was just as handsome as he had been last night, did not.

Had he known who I was last night? Had that been some sort of test or trick? Doubtful. He looked as surprised to see me as I was to see him.

"Hey, Harrison." Pops stood to shake his hand, then waved at me. "You remember my granddaughter, Winslow."

"Of course." Harrison took my hand as I stood, shaking it with a firm grip. "Welcome. We're glad to have you as our new chief of police."

"Thank you." My voice was surprisingly steady considering my heart was attempting to dive out of my chest and hide under the table. "I'm glad to be here."

"Would you like to join us?" Pops offered, nodding to the empty chairs at our table.

"No," Griffin said at the same time his father said, "We'd love to."

Neither Pops nor Harrison seemed to notice the tension rolling off Griffin's body as they took their chairs, leaving Griffin and me to introduce ourselves.

I swallowed hard, then extended a hand. "Hello."

That sharp jaw I'd traced with my tongue last night clenched so tight that I heard the crack of his molars. He glared at my hand before capturing it in his large palm. "Griffin."

Griffin Eden.

My one-night stand.

So much for serendipity.

## ABOUT THE AUTHOR

Devney Perry is a *Wall Street Journal* and *USA Today* bestselling author of over forty romance novels. After working in the technology industry for a decade, she abandoned conference calls and project schedules to pursue her passion for writing. She was born and raised in Montana and now lives in Washington with her husband and two sons.

Don't miss out on Devney's latest book news.
Subscribe to her newsletter!
www.devneyperry.com